Ellie's Magic Wish

igloobooks

I want to be a **fairy**
and sit on toadstools, drinking tea.

This igloo book belongs to:

....

igloobooks

Published in 2019
by Igloo Books Ltd
Cottage Farm
Sywell
NN6 0BJ
www.igloobooks.com

GUA006 1218
6 8 10 9 7 5
ISBN 978-1-78440-293-8

Illustrated by Kate Daubney
Written by Alice King

Printed and manufactured in China

I'll ask my other fairy friends to come and visit me.

If I were a fairy,
I'd have shiny, silky wings.
I'd flit around the forest
and twirl in fairy rings.

If I were a fairy,
I'd wave my magic wand.
I'd make a sparkly, golden boat
and sail around our pond.

If I were a fairy,
I'd make lots of magic wishes.

I'd make my bunny talk to me
and give me lots of kisses.

I want to be a **fairy** and have a secret den.

I'll sprinkle it with fairy dust and visit, now and then.

If I were a fairy,
I would meet the fairy queen.
She'd tell me that my pretty dress
was the best she'd ever seen.

I want to be a fairy
and dance to fairy tunes.

I'll be a fairy ballerina
and twirl under the moon.

If I were a fairy
I'd fly around at night.

I'd flit among the flowers
and shine my lantern light.

If I were a fairy,
I'd ride a magic unicorn.

He would glow like moonbeams
and have a golden horn.

I want to be a fairy
and make my wand go swish!

Maybe, if I'm very good,
one day I'll get my wish!

"Goodbye, see you soon!"